Story by Jennifer Trafton, Jonathan Rogers, and Randall Goodgame

Illustrations by Rickey Boyd, Color by Evan Csulik

Inspired by the episode *True Friendship* from *The Slugs & Bugs Show*
which can be streamed on RightNow Media.

Copyright 2020 Brentwood Studios, LLC.
Published by Brentwood Studios, Franklin TN in partnership with RightNow Media
ISBN# 978-1-7350996-2-0

This book has been produced using responsible and sustainably sourced paper

All rights reserved. Printed in Shenzhen, China - July 2020
1 2 3 4 5 • 24 23 22 21 20

brentwoodstudios.net

rightnowmedia.org

slugsandbugs.com

THE TALE OF THE LOST LURE

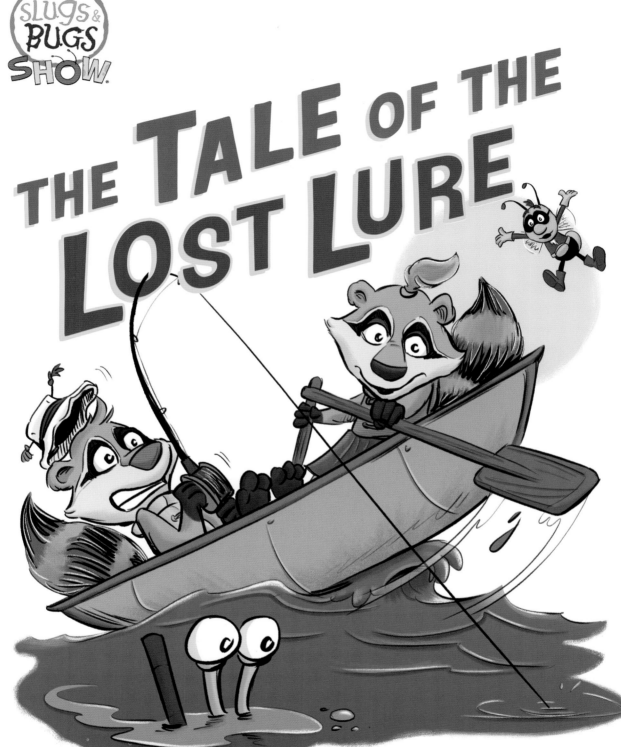

It was a slow day at the workshop, until . . .

"See you later, everybody," called Morty. "Chauncey let me borrow his lucky lure, so I'm going fishing at the pond!"

"The pond!?" all three friends replied with delight.

"I'm coming too!" said Maggie. "You'll need someone to row the boat."

First Morty fished the shallows, but the fish there weren't biting . . .

After a while, he cast the lure into the deepest part of the pond.

Suddenly, the line went tight.

"Morty! You caught a fish!"
cried Maggie.

Morty pulled.
"It's a big one!"

He pulled harder.
"A HUGE one!"
But the line
wouldn't budge.

"OH NO!" moaned Morty.

"Sorry bud. The Zorbian submarine must have snapped your line."

"No, Doug's right," said Maggie. "The lure probably got caught on a log—"

"Or a lake monster," said Doug.

They looked over the edge of the boat into the water, but all they could see was swirling blue.

Morty groaned. He had lost the lucky lure! He couldn't stand the thought of disappointing Chauncy.

The lure was out there *somewhere* (along with maybe a lake monster).

There was clearly only one thing to do.

Morty leaped.

Sparky grabbed his tail. "Stop!"

"The pond is deep, and you can't hold your breath that long!" yelled Maggie.

"But Maggie, I have to find that lure!"

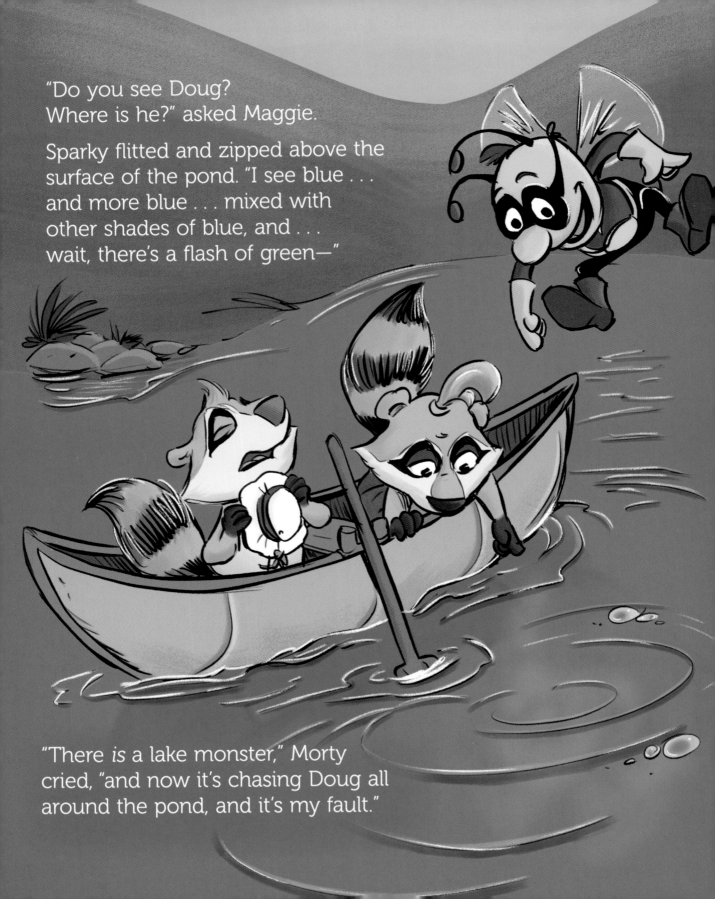

"Do you see Doug?
Where is he?" asked Maggie.

Sparky flitted and zipped above the
surface of the pond. "I see blue . . .
and more blue . . . mixed with
other shades of blue, and . . .
wait, there's a flash of green—"

"There *is* a lake monster," Morty
cried, "and now it's chasing Doug all
around the pond, and it's my fault."

"No, wait. Never mind. That's just my reflection," said Sparky.

"Look what I found!"

"My whizbee!" said Maggie. "I lost it in the pond last spring!"

"Did you find the lure?" asked Morty.

"Not yet," said Doug, and he dove back down again.

"What about the lure? Did you find the lure?"

"Not yet," said Doug, and he dove back down again.

The sun began to sink, and so did Morty's hopes. "Maybe Chauncy will forget to ask for his lucky lure back, and I could save up lots of money and buy him a new one."

Maggie looked doubtful.

"Or maybe I could tell him we were stopped by a rowdy gang of lure robbers and—and—and—"

"But Morty," said Maggie, "that would be lying. We're supposed to be *reformed* raccoons. And you're worrying so much you're rocking the whole boat!"

"Okay, okay," Morty said miserably. "Let's go back. I'll tell him the truth. But—but what if Chauncy never trusts me with anything again? What if Doug gets gobbled up by the lake monster, and it's all my fault? What if—"

"Morty," Maggie interrupted. "*What if* . . . instead of imagining *bad* things and getting all worked up, you used your imagination to think of *good* things? Then you could be *hoping* instead of *moping*."

"Just because it rhymes doesn't mean it's easy," Morty muttered.

"Imagine this, Morty!" called Sparky. "The Electric Elf peers through the mucky pond with his lightning vision, blinding the terrible lake monster as a brave slug narrowly escapes—"

"You're not helping, Sparky," sighed Maggie.

Morty was true to his word, and when they got back to the workshop, he told Chauncey everything.

"I'm sorry, Chauncy. I understand if you don't want to let me borrow anything special again."

But Chauncy didn't scowl or scold. He threw his arms around his son and laughed! "Do you know how many lures I've lost in that pond? Enough to catch all the fish in the ocean! Accidents happen to the best of us, Morty. But thank you for telling me the truth."

"So you're not angry with me?"

"Not a bit."

"Which one is the lucky lure?" asked Morty.

Chauncy laughed so hard they thought his cheeks might explode.

"Whichever one I'm still lucky enough to have! I told you I've lost a lot of lures in that pond! I think we should celebrate by going fishing tomorrow.

What do you think, Morty?

"Oops!"

Story inspired by

The Bible
John 13:34-35
Proverbs 16:13

The Music
Love One Another by Slugs & Bugs
God Makes Messy Things Beautiful by Slugs & Bugs

The TV Episode
True Friendship from The Slugs & Bugs Show